The adventures of

Rosie and William

Text by
Rosalie Kuyvenhoven

Illustrations by
Annemarieke Kloosterhof

For Lena and Chiem

The most beautiful place on earth
is the world
of your imagination.

Content

Night

It's night-time.
The moon is round.
The stars are twinkling.
There are over a million of them.
'Right to the end of the numbers,' Rosie would say.

Rosie is six years old.
Her favourite colour is blue, the colour of her eyes.
She loves to draw, and in her imagination
absolutely anything can happen.
Sometimes she asks clever questions.
Questions which even mummy and daddy
find tricky to answer.

Rosie is lying in bed with Mister Monkey,
her favourite cuddly toy.
She is dreaming that she has long hair,
just like a princess.
She plucks a star from the sky
and they dance together.

Rosie's brother sleeps in the room next to hers.
His name is William. William is three years old.
He is very good at pretending to be all sorts of vehicles:
racing cars, fire-engines, trains, even aeroplanes!

William's favourite colour is red,
just like his favourite superhero's outfit.
Foxy, his very best cuddly toy friend,
is purring away next to him.

William is also dreaming.
He is wearing his red superhero costume.
He is flying as fast as a rocket:
straight through the clouds,
all the way to the moon.
Hello moon! The moon smiles at William.

Then, in the distance, you can hear
the bells of the clock tower.
One, two, three, four, five, six.
The sun rises. The moon disappears.
One by one the stars dim their lights.

Rosie and William's rooms fill with sunlight.
The day begins.

William's nose

It's very early in the morning.
William opens his eyes.
The house is still quiet.

William gets up out of bed
and walks out of his room.

Suddenly, he freezes.
What's that over there?

In the mirror, a little boy is looking at him.
He looks just like William:
he, too, has blond hair and brown eyes.
But there is something odd about this little boy:
he doesn't have a nose!
Now that is strange.

William searches for his own nose with his hand.
The little boy also moves his hand to his face.
But what's this?
William can't feel his nose!
His nose is gone.

William decides to look for his nose.
He softly tiptoes downstairs.
Perhaps his cuddly toys can help.

'Hello Kitty Cat,' William says.
'Have you seen my nose?'
'No,' purrs Kitty Cat.
'But you can borrow mine if you like.'
And suddenly, William has whiskers!

There is Mister Duck.
'Hello Mister Duck,' William says.
'Have you seen my nose?'
'No,' quacks Mister Duck.
'But you can borrow mine if you like.'
And suddenly, William has a beak!

Ellie Elephant wakes up too.
'Hello Ellie Elephant,' William says.
'Have you seen my nose?'
'No,' Ellie Elephant trumpets.
'But you can borrow mine if you like.'
And suddenly, William has a trunk!

Finally, Foxy comes to take a look.
'Hello Foxy,' William says.
'Have you seen my nose?'
'No,' sniffs Foxy.
'But you can borrow mine if you like.'
And suddenly, William has a fox's
snout!

William is having a lot of fun wearing all these noses.
But he still wants his own nose back.
He can smell best with it,
and pick it best, too.

All this searching for his nose has made William tired.
He crawls back into bed.
Joined by his cuddly toys:
Kitty Cat, Mister Duck, Ellie Elephant and Foxy.
He falls asleep.

When the morning sun shines through his window,
William wakes up.
His cuddly toys are sitting up straight in bed.
They are pointing at William's face.
'It's back!'

William carefully touches his face.
'Hurray! It's back! My nose is back!'
Excited, William jumps out of bed.
He can't wait to tell mummy and daddy
about his great nose adventure!

Nowhere

Rosie wakes up.
She has had a really good sleep.
And yet she feels a little bit strange.
She goes to see mummy.

'Mummy, when I was asleep,
it felt as if I was nowhere.
Where are you when you're nowhere?'

Mummy gives Rosie a big cuddle.
'Good morning sweetheart.
Now, where are you when you're nowhere?
That is a pretty tricky question.
What do you think?'

'I don't know,' says Rosie.
'Maybe you're just - not there?'

Mummy thinks about it for a bit.
'When you're asleep you are still there.
But you're completely calm.
You don't see or hear anything.
And you sort of forget that you're there.

But, you can still have lots of adventures
when you're asleep.
Did you have a dream?'

'Yes,' says Rosie.
'I dreamt that I was a princess.
And that I lived in a castle.'

'Anything can happen in your dreams,' mummy says.
'And in your dreams you can be wherever you want to be.
So when you're asleep it seems like you're nowhere,
but, actually, you're everywhere!'

Baby

William has a baby in his tummy.
'Mummy, would you like to feel my baby?'
Mummy would love to.

Gently, she rubs William's tummy.
'Hello baby,' she says quietly.
'Is it nice and cosy there, in William's tummy?'

'In a little bit, the baby's going to be born,'
William says.
'Then he will come out of my tummy. Look, like this.'

William lifts his jumper.
The baby's tiny head is already showing.
And there is his body.
And his little feet.

Proudly, William holds up his baby.
The baby has a cheerful little face.
And funny ears.
He has black beady eyes.
His skin is red and fluffy.

'What's your baby's name?' asks mummy.
William takes a good look at his new baby.
'Foxy,' William says.
'My baby's name is Foxy.'
And he gives Foxy a gentle kiss.

Foxy's journey

William is very sad.
Foxy is lost.
His sweet, soft, beautiful little Foxy.
Gone.

They woke up together just this morning.
They ate porridge and bread.
Everything seemed fine.

Now it's night-time
and William wants to go to sleep.
But Foxy's missing.
Foxy has disappeared.

Just like that.
Without a 'goodbye',
without a kiss,
and without even leaving a message.

A day goes by.
And another one.
A week goes by.
And another one.

William plays with his other cuddly toys now.
But none of them can replace Foxy.
'Foxy, where are you?'
But nobody answers.

Then,
one day,
a letter drops onto the doormat.

'Dear William,' the letter begins.
'I'm so sorry I haven't been in touch.
I went on a journey.
But now I'm coming back, because I miss you.
I would like to play with you again, please.
Bye!
Foxy.'

William dances around the house.
'Foxy! I got a letter from Foxy!'

The next day the doorbell rings.
William runs to the door.
It's the postman.
He is holding a large box.

'I have a delivery for William,' the postman says.
'Does he live here?'
'Yes!' shouts William.
'That's me!'

The postman hands the large box to William.
From inside it, William can hear
a familiar little growl.
Quickly, he opens the box.
Two beady black eyes are looking up at him.

'Hello William!' says Foxy.
'I'm so happy to see you again!'

William cuddles Foxy as tightly as he can.
'Please don't ever do that again, Foxy.
Leave just like that, without taking me with you.'

'I'll never do it again,' Foxy says.
'Besides, it was no fun without you.
Come on, let's play.
I'll be your baby and you can be my daddy.'
And so they do.

Mermaid

Rosie is in the swimming pool.
She's having a great time.
Swimming is fun!

Rosie is playing a diving game.
She throws a ring to
the bottom of the pool.
There goes the ring.
She watches it sink slowly.

Rosie takes a deep breath.
She takes a look at the water
and dives in.
It's very quiet underwater.
The light shimmers
on the bottom of the pool.

Rosie takes long strokes
and swims all the way down.

She looks at her legs.
Where her feet used to be
she now sees a beautiful tail.

Her legs have scales on them.
She has red curly hair
with little shells in it.
Rosie has become a mermaid!

A little further along, she spots a beautiful castle.
Rosie swims towards it.
The castle has a large gate.
A seahorse comes to open the door for her.

Rosie enters a large hallway.
She sees a prince.

'Welcome darling Rosie,' the prince says.
'Are you perhaps looking for this?'
The prince hands Rosie a ring.
It's the ring she threw to the bottom of the pool.

'Yes,' says Rosie.
'That's mine, thank you.'
And she gives the prince a kiss.

'You had better hurry back up,' the prince says.
'Before your mummy starts to worry.
Will you come back soon?'
Rosie promises that she will.

She waves at the prince, and swims away.
Out of the hall.
Through the gate.
Towards the light.

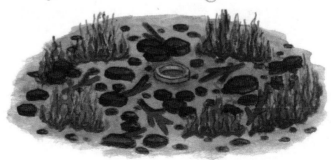

Crocodile

The doorbell rings.
Excitedly, Rosie and William run to the front door.
Who could it be?
'Tadaaa... surprise!'
It's Uncle Chris!

'Hi guys! Look what I brought!'
'A crocodile?' Rosie and William ask surprisedly.
'Indeed, a crocodile. I ran into him at sea.
He wanted to see where you live.'

'May we come in?
I'm pretty hungry after that long journey,'
the crocodile says.
He walks inside, past Rosie and William.
He is even taller than Uncle Chris!

Rosie and William are a little frightened of the crocodile.
In fact, they're pretty shocked: a crocodile has come to visit!

The crocodile sits down at the table.
Uncle Chris makes a cup of tea.
Rosie and William get lemonade.

'I baked cookies,' Rosie says.
'Would you like some?'
And so together they enjoy a nice cup of tea and lemonade.
With cookies.

Rosie and William are allowed to climb
on the crocodile's back.
And they're allowed to tickle his tummy.

They even take a bath with the crocodile.
They sing a song:
'Bubbles, bubbles everywhere,
splash it here and splash it there!'

The crocodile gets to sleep in the big bed with Rosie.
She's never had such a huge cuddly toy in her bed before.

The next day, Uncle Chris and the crocodile leave again.
Back to sea.

The crocodile cries a little.
He had such a good time!

Deflated

William, Rosie, mummy and daddy are in a restaurant.
It's lunchtime.
William has ordered a cheese sandwich.
He picks up a napkin.

'Mummy, would you please fold me a hat?'
Mummy says she will.
William hands mummy his napkin.
Mummy folds the napkin into a hat.
He puts it on his head.
Now he looks just like a pirate!

William picks up his knife and fork.
He starts to play with his fork.
'Careful now,' daddy says.
'Before you know it, you'll prick a hole in your hand.
And then you'll deflate.'

But it's too late.
Pffffffff!
William has pricked a tiny hole.
He's got a puncture.

He shoots upward, like a balloon.
William gets caught on a lamp.
He looks down, where he sees
mummy, daddy and Rosie looking up with a fright.

'Ahoy!' shouts William.

He has a great view from the lamp.
It's like a crow's nest on a ship.
William explores the view.
He can see the kitchen
in the distance.
The cook is making
a cheese sandwich.
That must be for William!

And, yes.
The waiter picks up the sandwich.
He walks right over
to William's table.

William jumps down.
He lands on his chair.
But he is still deflated!
He can't eat like this.

'Hang on,' daddy says.
'I'll re-inflate you.'
And so he does.
He finds William's valve,
and he blows and blows and blows.

William is inflated again.
He picks up his fork.
But this time it's just for
pricking his sandwich with.
Yum!

Eraser

Rosie is drawing a picture.
She draws a horse and a sun.
The head of the horse isn't working out so well.

Rosie grabs the eraser.
She rubs and rubs.
The horse disappears.
But so does the paper.

Rosie keeps on rubbing.
Now the table disappears too,
as well as the chair she's sitting on.

There comes William,
with screaming sirens.
Rosie also rubs out William,
as well as his fire-engine.

Soon, Rosie has rubbed out the entire house.
She keeps on rubbing.
The garden disappears,
the street, her school.

When the eraser has run out,
Rosie looks around.

The world is completely white and empty.

Rosie picks up her colouring pencils
and begins to draw a whole new world of her own.
She draws bright pink grass.
A field full of it.

She draws a little flower.
And another.
Rosie draws
over a hundred flowers.

Then she draws a horse.
A horse with pretty
braided manes.

Rosie draws a castle.
The castle has big, tall towers
and a large drawbridge.
It's the most beautiful
castle in the world.

Then she draws three little girls.
Happy girls, with rosy cheeks.

Rosie is a little hungry.
She draws a great big cake
with whipped cream and strawberries.

Rosie dances with her three new friends
in the field full of flowers.

They eat cake, as much as they can.
Then they climb on the horse's back.
The horse takes the girls,
through the bright pink grass,
to the castle.

There must be over a hundred rooms in the castle.
With heavenly beds and fluffy cushions.
They play hide and seek.
The horse loses.

They blow big bubbles out of soap and air.
And they live happily ever after.

Stone

William is lying on mummy and daddy's bed.
He is a stone.
He cannot move.
He cannot see.
He cannot hear.

'William! Where are you?
Come out, come out, wherever you are!
Time to get dressed.'
Daddy is looking for William.
But William the stone is not moving.
He's just fine where he is.

Daddy enters the bedroom.
'Oh, here you are! Come along.'

'I'm a stone.
I can't move,' says William.

'Well, would you believe it, a talking stone,'
daddy says.
'How very interesting!
Shall I tickle this stone?
Or maybe I should give it a raspberry?'

Daddy starts to walk towards the bed.
Towards William the stone.
'No!' screams William.
He jumps up.
And he launches himself off the bed,
and out of the room.

Like a rock-et!

Creepy crawlies

William is in the garden.
He is lying on his tummy in the tall grass.
He is looking at the creepy crawlies.

There is a snail.
It has a little house on its back.
Ever so slowly, the snail creeps forward.
It's leaving sticky slime behind.

William finds its feelers funny.
He touches them with a small stick.
But it shocks the snail.
It quickly hides away in its little house.
And gone is the snail.

William gets up.
There are ants!
More than William can count:
One, two, three, four, eight, eleven...

William sees a big ant bearing a bit of bread on its back.
That's a strong ant!
William follows the ant.
It's creeping towards a little hole in the wall.
And gone is the ant.

Then William sees a tiny red creepy crawly on a leaf.
It has black dots on its wings.
He lets the creepy crawly walk along his finger.
It tickles.

Suddenly the creepy crawly grows wings.
It flies off.
And gone is the ladybird.

Suddenly William feels a drop on his nose.
And another one.
It's raining.
William quickly goes inside the house.
And gone is William.

Nose-picking

William puts his finger up his nose.
Is there anything tasty in there?

'Hey nose-picker! There aren't any biscuits up there!'
Oh no, he's been caught out.

Mummy doesn't think it's proper
for William to pick his nose.
'I'm only pretending,' William explains.

When mummy's gone,
William puts his finger back up his nose.
Maybe he could fit two fingers in at once?

William looks in the mirror.
Yes, he can: his forefinger in the right nostril
and his middle finger in the left one.
That looks funny!

Picking your nose is fun, and tasty too.
Mummy is completely wrong.

There may not be any biscuits up William's nose,
but there are marshmallows,
and wine gums, and jelly babies too!

Yummy!

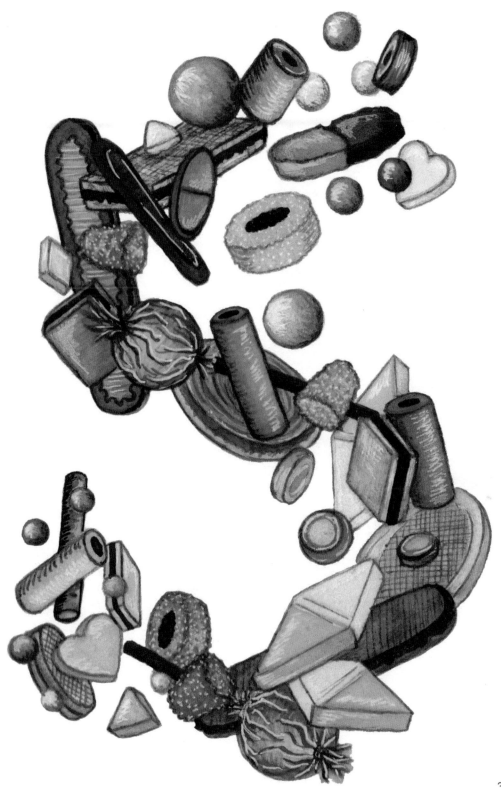

In a bit

'Mum?'
'Hmmmm?'
'Will you come play with me?'
'Just a minute, love.
I'm just in the middle of writing this email.
But if you go ahead and find us a game to play,
I'll be right with you.'

Rosie walks over to the toy cabinet.
Which game should she pick?
Guessing faces, that's a fun one!

Rosie walks back to mummy.
'I've found a game. Look.
Now will you come and play with me?'

But then mummy's phone rings.
'Just a minute love, I'll be there in a bit.
I really must take this phone call.
But if you go ahead and set up the game,
I'll be right with you.'

Rosie sighs.
Mummy never comes right away!
It's always 'in a bit'.

She sets up the board game
and picks out a nice face.
Maria! She likes that one.

'I'm ready, mum! Will you come play now?'
Finally, mummy puts the phone down.
She walks over to Rosie.

Mummy, too, picks out a face.
But then she looks at the clock.
'Oh Rosie! Is it that late already?
We have to go and pick up William from playschool!
Come along, put your shoes on, quickly.'

Rosie sighs.
But suddenly, she comes up with a plan:
'In a bit', two can play that game!

And Rosie says:
'Just a minute, mum.
I'm just in the middle of this game!
But if you go on ahead and put on your coat,
I'll be right with you.'

Tweedle-dee-dum

'Are you coming to my concert?'
Rosie walks into the kitchen.
She is holding her violin.
'It's about to start!'

Mummy, daddy and William follow Rosie
into the living room, where the concert will be.
'Hold on,' Rosie says.
'You have to buy a ticket first.'

Rosie puts her violin in its case.
She gets out three sheets of paper.
She has drawn a violin and a musical note on each of them.
Rosie has also written names on them:
daddy, mummy and William.

'That'll be twenty pence a ticket, please,' says Rosie.
Mummy, daddy and William each buy a ticket.
They choose a nice spot in the concert hall.

Rosie picks up her violin and bow.
She looks at her audience.
'Welcome to the concert!
I am going to play a song.
It's called: Tweedle-dee-dum.'

Rosie places the violin under her chin.
She takes a good look at her music sheet.

It has notes on it, and a pretty picture.
A picture of an animal orchestra.

She sees a frog with a flute,
a beetle with a double bass,
a duck with a drum,
a turtle with a tambourine,
a chicken with a cello,
a cuckoo with a clarinet
and a badger with a banjo.
The conductor is a toad.

The toad lifts up his baton.
'Rosie, pay attention! We're about to begin!'
Rosie places her bow on the E-string.
The toad taps the beat.

Rosie starts to play.
And the entire orchestra joins in:
E-E-E, AAA, E-E-E, AAA...
Twee-dle-dee-dum, Twee-dle-dee-dum...
It sounds absolutely beautiful!

Rosie closes her eyes.
This way she can hear the music even better.
She plays the whole piece by heart.
After the final note there is a short pause.

But then the audience begins to clap very loudly.
'Beautiful!' shouts mummy.
'Again!' shouts daddy.
'Hurray!' shouts William.

Rosie is a bit embarrassed by the applause.
She bows as deeply as she possibly can.
Giving a concert is fun!

Tidying

'This place is a total tip!
I am throwing everything out!'
Oh no! Daddy is in one of his tidying moods.
Ring the alarm bells!

Rosie and William rush to protect their toys.
Their cars, their cuddly toys, their arts and crafts things,
and all of the other stuff that they play with often,
or even not so often: everything is in danger!

Here comes daddy. He's carrying a large bag.
He is on the hunt.

'Ha! A cuddly toy!
You have about seventy-five of those.
We can get rid of at least forty-five.'
And he stuffs one of Rosie's bears into the bag.

'Nooooo!' Rosie screams at the top of her lungs.
Not that bear! That's my favourite!'
And she tugs at the bag.
She can hear the little bear softly crying inside the bag.

Daddy continues his hunt.
'Cars!
You also have at least one-hundred-and-eighty of those.
Away with them!'
And he puts a handful of cars into the bag.

'Nooooo!' William charges towards daddy.
'You put my red racing car in there.
You can't get rid of that!'

Daddy looks at Rosie and William.
He, too, can hear the bear crying.
'Alright,' he says.
'I have an idea.

Together, we are going to collect one bagful of toys.
Toys that you haven't played with in a long time.
We will take those toys to the charity shop.
That way you can make other children happy with them.'

Daddy takes the bear and the car back out of the bag.
Rosie cuddles the bear tightly.
William quickly puts the car safely into his pocket.

Rosie and William go through all of their toys with daddy.
It turns out that they do have some toys
that they no longer play with.

A rattle for a baby.
A puzzle they never finish.
Four dusty cuddly toys.
Dress-up clothes that no longer fit.
And a few broken cars.
The bag is full!

Rosie, William and daddy go to the charity shop.
They give the bag to the charity shop lady.
'Thank you!' the lady says enthusiastically.
She takes the toys out of the bag.

'I think you've done a brilliant job.
Do you know what?
You can choose something from the shop in return.'

Wow!
Rosie and William look around.
They see a nice big puzzle.
They would like that one.
It fits perfectly inside the empty bag.

'But...,' daddy protests.
Rosie and William give him their sweetest look.
And so they return home.
With a very full bag.

Baby sister

Rosie is walking down the street with mummy.
She squeezes mummy's hand.
'Mummy, I want you and daddy
to cuddle really well tonight.'
'That sounds nice,' mummy says.
'Why do you want that so badly?'

'I want a baby,' Rosie says.
'If you cuddle really well, then just maybe,
if you're lucky, you get a baby.
That's what daddy told me.'

Mummy laughs.
'And would you like a baby sister
or a baby brother then?' asks mummy.
'A baby sister,' Rosie answers immediately.
'Because I don't like boys very much.'
'Then we must think of a name,' says mummy.
'What is the baby sister going to be called?'

But Rosie already has a plan.
'I think that I should be allowed to choose the name,
because it was my idea.
And it has to be a name that rhymes with Rosie.'

Rosie thinks out loud:
'Posie, Crosie, Toesie, Wissywosie...'
No, those aren't very good names for a baby sister.

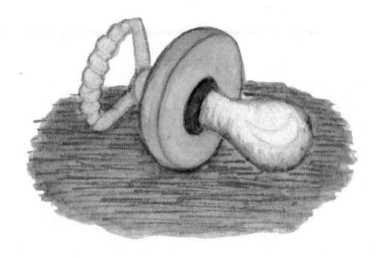

Rosie's brains are creaking away.
And then she has a solution.

'You know what, mummy, I think we should have twins.
And then I will call them Lilly and Billy.
Is that a good idea?'
Rosie looks at mummy expectantly.

'Whew,' says mummy.
'I think two babies would be a bit much.
But I'd be alright with one.
Daddy would have to want a new baby too, though.'
'Then I will go and ask him in a bit,' says Rosie.

Rosie and mummy have returned home.
Daddy is cooking.
He is tasting to see whether his sauce is any good.
Rosie runs towards him.

'Daddy, I want to have a baby sister.
May I?
Then you have to cuddle mummy tonight.'

Daddy nearly chokes on the sauce.
'A baby sister?
You and William already make plenty of noise
and arguments as it is.
No, I think we're just fine as we are.

But cuddling mummy does sound like a good idea.
And I also love to cuddle my favourite little girl!'

Daddy picks Rosie up and gives her a big kiss.

Secret

Rosie, William, mummy and daddy are sitting at the table.

Rosie raises her hand.
'Quiet guys,' daddy says. 'Rosie wants to say something.'
Mummy, daddy and William look at Rosie.

'I know a secret,' says Rosie.
Her eyes twinkle.
'It is a very special secret
and you're not allowed to tell anyone.'

Mummy, daddy and William are very curious.
'What's the secret?' mummy asks.
Rosie sits up straight.
She looks them all in the eye, one by one.

'When a baby smiles for the first time,
a fairy is born.'
Mummy, daddy and William have gone really quiet.
Rosie continues.

'When the baby smiles,
a tiny bit of fluff floats off a wishing flower.
The wind blows the tiny bit of fluff to the fairy queen.'
Rosie pretends to be the wind.

She presses her lips together and blows softly.

'Then the fairy queen sprinkles tiny golden stars
over the piece of fluff.'
Rosie's hands swirl through the air.
Suddenly, the room gets a little brighter.
'And then,' Rosie continues secretively,
'then the piece of fluff turns into a fairy.'

William, daddy and mummy all hold their breath.
They think it's a beautiful story.
'The little fairy then protects the baby,' Rosie explains.
'Whenever the baby is sad, the fairy tells a joke.
The fairy always stays with the baby.
Even when the baby grows up.'

William thinks for a bit.
'Do I also have a fairy?' he asks.
'Yes,' Rosie says.
'Everyone has a fairy.'

William looks around him.
'But I can't see it!'

'That's because fairies are a secret,' Rosie says.
'You can't see them, but they're really there.
Just close your eyes and see.'

William, mummy and daddy close their eyes.
It's very quiet.
Nothing.
But then, suddenly, they hear something.
A soft rustling noise, like a whisper.
The secret of the fairies.

Dinner

Daddy puts a plate of food in front of William.
William looks at his plate.
He sees green things.
They are long and thin,
and they have brown spots on them.
What are these disgusting creatures?

William examines what else is on his plate.
He sees long ribbons.
They look like worms.
They are covered in some sort of mush.
A red mush with strange bits in it.
William makes a face.
He pushes the plate away.
'I don't like thi-i-is.'

Daddy looks at him.
'They're runner beans, William.
And spaghetti bolognese.
It's delicious!'
And daddy takes a large bite of food from his own plate.

But William turns around in his chair.
He folds his arms angrily.
'You never make what I like!' he yells angrily.

Then he hears a noise.

'Teeeee-dooooo, teeeeee-dooooo!
This fire-engine is looking for a mouth!'

William sees a bite of red coming his way.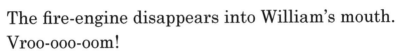
It does look a little like a fire-engine.
He should help this fire-engine out!
And he opens his mouth.
Munch.

The fire-engine disappears into William's mouth.
Vroo-ooo-oom!
Here comes a lorry
… and a plane
… and a train
… and a police car
… and a bus
… and an ambulance
… and a rocket
… and a forklift truck
… and a digger.

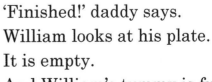
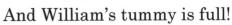

'Finished!' daddy says.
William looks at his plate.
It is empty.
And William's tummy is full!

Handbag

Mummy and daddy are going out on a date.
Rosie looks at mummy.
Mummy is wearing a beautiful dress.
She is wearing high heels and lipstick.
Rosie thinks mummy looks very pretty.

She has an idea.
'Wait a minute mummy,' Rosie says.
And she runs upstairs,
to her room.

A moment later, she returns.
She is holding a handbag.
It's a pink handbag, which glitters.
It has a picture of a little girl on it.
It's Rosie's most treasured handbag.

'Mummy, do you want to borrow this one?
You can if you like.
But you have to make sure you don't lose it
and that it doesn't get stolen.'

Mummy looks at Rosie.
'How sweet! I would love to borrow your handbag.
I'll take very good care of it.'
Mummy puts her purse and keys in the handbag.

Now she looks even prettier.
She waves goodbye to Rosie and William.
'Sweet dreams, see you in the morning!'
Rosie and William wave back.
'Bye! Have fun!'

Rosie looks at her handbag in mummy's hand.
The little girl in the picture is looking at her.
She winks at Rosie.
And Rosie winks back.

The orange balloon

Rosie is lying in bed.
Daddy has read her a bedtime story
and given her a cuddle.
'Sweet dreams, little girl.'

Rosie is lying in bed.
Mummy has given her a drink to help her fall asleep
and kissed her goodnight.
'Sweet dreams, little girl.'

Rosie is lying in bed.
But she can't sleep.
The voices in her head won't quiet down.

Rosie turns on the light.
She picks up a book and reads a little.
But the voices won't stop talking.
'Stop, voices!' Rosie shouts.

Then she picks up Mister Monkey.
She gives Mister Monkey a cuddle
and puts him beside her under the duvet.
'Sweet dreams, Mister Monkey!'

Rosie lies back down again.
Next to Mister Monkey.
But the voices still won't be quiet.
Stupid voices!

Mummy comes into Rosie's room.
'Are you still awake?'
'Yes mummy,' Rosie says.
'The voices in my head won't stop talking.'

Mummy lies down next to Rosie.
'Shall we send the voices away?
Just shut your eyes
and try to breathe very calmly.'

Rosie lies down. On her back.
She breathes in and out.
Her belly is going up and down with each breath.

'We are going to send the voices away with a balloon,'
mummy says. 'You can pick a colour.'
'Orange,' says Rosie.
'The balloon is going to be orange.'
'Good!' says mummy.

'Take a good look at that orange balloon.
What does it look like?'

Rosie looks carefully at the balloon in her head.
'It's big.
Because there are lots of voices
and they all have to fit in.'

'Good,' says mummy.
'And what shape does the balloon have?'
'It's the shape of my head.
Because that will make the voices think
they're inside my head!'

'That's clever of you,' mummy says.
'Is the balloon finished now?'

'It also has a rope attached to it,' Rosie says.
'That way it looks like the balloon has a neck.
Just like me.'

'Okay,' says mummy.
'Now we are going to put all the voices inside the balloon.
Are you ready?

Rosie gathers all of the little voices in her head.
She blows and she blows.
Pffff... pffff... pffff...

One by one she blows the voices into the orange balloon.
It becomes bigger and bigger.
Pffff... pffff... pffff...

Rosie can feel herself calming down.

'Are all the voices inside the balloon?' mummy asks.
'Then tie the balloon shut very tightly with the rope.
That way they won't be able to get back out.'

Rosie ties the rope in a pretty bow.
Then she slowly lets go of the balloon.
Quietly, the balloon floats away,
across Rosie's bed, past her bedside lamp,
and out through the open window.

Rosie watches the balloon fly away.
It becomes quiet inside her head.
It becomes quiet in her room.

Rosie is asleep.

First print, 2016

Translated from Dutch. Original title 'De avonturen van Rosa en Willem'
Text © 2015 Rosalie Kuyvenhoven
Illustrations © 2015 Annemarieke Kloosterhof

Cover illustration Annemarieke Kloosterhof
Design Studio Kuyvenhoven
Translation Vertaalbureau Textwerk

Publisher Orange Balloon Books
www.orangeballoonbooks.com

ISBN 978-90-824171-1-1

Made in the USA
Charleston, SC
21 January 2016